Through the Years

When one has thousands of pages of words some maybe should be shared, not as a history, but more of love and Christian inspiration. Each heading will be less a story and more that of prose that carries with it thoughts that you might have had yourself. I might offer that the best way to take on these words would be with a soft light and a warm cup of tea or coffee and a prayer.

Happy Reading

Mike Kelley

Table of Contents

One:

A Broken Day

A day broken in loss brings a shattered night

Hands fold looking for the words

Prayers to a God who already knows

Someone slipped away hiding in the devils' arms

Fires of blame you light

Blame in yourself

Even one life is too much to lose

The letting go too painful

You find tears wishing to wash away the pain

Then at your lowest point comes a hand

God has been with you all the way

He listened to the words of your prayers

Words of hope you tried to give to ears that would not hear

To eyes that would not see

Everyone has a choice it is not your failing

You were sent to be an example

To open doors to a soul

A door chosen to be locked in evil

God holds you not accounting

The sad reality awakens within your broken heart

You tried

Take courage and try again

Fight as long as you have life

Pray with passion

Reach out to another

Always reaching out

Keep your eyes to the horizons of God

You are a worker in his labors

May God bless your fighting faith

Be restored in the next tomorrow

Pick up the cross and realized that Jesus has walked the same path

Two:

The Voice

A voice from somewhere

Calls from places beyond

Ghost, some

Spirits, some

God, all

A voice moves my thoughts

Taking me to his place

That holy spot

Light brightens the way

"Son of man he calls"

"Yes" I answer

"Hear me and follow"

We walk through the world together

"See" he points

"Yes" I answer

Behold there is darkness and evil in the path

Screams, cries, and death

Sickness, loneliness, lust, and hate

Darkness filled with robbers, killers, and cheaters of mankind

Lawlessness

Commandment breakers of the ten

These of the devils' army at war

Fighting forces of the demons

“Son of man he calls”

“Yes” I answer

“Step into the evil with goodness” he commands

“Do not be afraid” he says, “I am with you”

“Are you ready?” he asks

“Yes” I answer

“Son of man he calls”

“Go and bring the good news in the face of all evil”

“Go to the darkness with your light”

"Go now"

"Yes" I answer

Stepping into the filth of the earth, across the trail of blood, against all forces of the devil, my faith holds me on course

Now as I walk telling of the good news of Jesus, I hear footsteps with me

Turning, I am not alone for I am one of the armies of the Christians

Together we have taken on all the evil ahead

We overcome some, other will not be swayed

We judge not, and bring Jesus to forgive their sins

As he has forgiven us, when God calls will you join?

Three:

Another Midnight Hour

Another Midnight Hour
That outside world is quite
The darkness softens
This is the time of moonlight
Breaking from the hold of clouds
Sending down a glow
Shadows cast lightly across my window
Peace sings in such to me
Others sleep as dreams unfold
I awake lift prayers for dreams given
Thanks for blessings
Oh, other prayers too
Prayers for friends, and family always
Prayers for maybe you
Yes, we have never met, but I pray for you
I pray for goodness in this life

Maybe it will be you to bring
I pray for peace to share
Maybe it will be you to make
I pray for you in so many ways
Maybe God will tell you so
I pray words to guide us both
Maybe not by moonlight that fades
I pray that you become the light
Maybe one that shines day and night
I pray for you, and I pray for me
Maybe now our paths may cross
I pray someday they do
Maybe you pray for me too
I pray for us who face a world of hate
Maybe you and I can change it with love
I pray for us to our God above
Maybe one little heart will turn
I pray for another midnight hour

Maybe something good to pray into a new tomorrow

For this I pray

Maybe you pray it too

I fold my hands in the shadow of the moon

I pray for you my unknown friend

In Jesus name, I pray you now a peaceful night

A-Men

Four:

Big Chief

Big Chief

Back in the days of long ago

When eyes were clear, and life seemed full of adventure

Back when school was the starting place in life

Grade School with all the things of learning

The Crayola crayons that got me in trouble for melting them on the steam radiator that smelled up my first-grade classroom

That little jar of paste that I ate more than used

That fat round pencil with no eraser

That Big chief writing tablet, who would have thought of Native Americans would give such a prize

The pages had lines spaced apart and in the early years we learned to write our A-B-Cs inside those spaces

Those early school supplies had a fragrance to them all, one I still love

Finger paint, now that was fun but a bit messy

My artwork was not to hang anywhere but maybe mom would keep it in a dresser drawer for a time

The wooden rulers were weapons used by the teachers to keep you quiet in class, (never worked for me)

Then it happened, my first ever story written to the lines of that Big Chief tablet. It was about a horse that could change sizes and fit into my pocket or to ride on when made large again

Well today it would not seem like much maybe, but back in those early days of school my teacher took notice and wrote a note home to my parents, (This time not about talking in class too much, or eating paste, or melting crayons) it was to make note of the thinking to write it with such imagination, I was always quick with a lie at home, but this was different

Mom kept that story and the note from my teacher, Ms. Cox, in a metal box of special papers and I guess it got lost in time

Today I do not have a Big Chief tablet to write on, times have changed so much since then and we have lost the joy of smearing words spelled wrong with spit, then trying to write over them in darker letters

By the time I made it to the Navy growing up I was using a Remington Rand typewriter, still spelling words wrong, and erasing them leaving holes in the page from those early type erasers

Now all these years later still spelling things wrong I have learned the joy of (Spell Check) on my computer and using a writing program that keeps telling me to write things the way I do not talk, so in most cases I just keep going on with my Kentucky slang

Today I have thousands on thousands of pages of words written, none will bring me fame or glory, but they all have allowed me to express somethings that is inside me that cries to get out

As now a Christian writer I still have that same call but now I have become the hand of a greater power one that directs words to the page

I wonder if God has a big storeroom with that paste I used to eat, the crayons I loved to melt, Those big round pencils without erasers, and maybe a few tablets with Big Chief on the cover

Five:

Buckeye Thunderstorm

Buckeye Thunderstorm

Loveland, Ohio

Flashing Lightning

Nature sings its song

Waters dance in puddles

Puddles flood into ripples

The Little Miami River drinks in with a thirsty happy flow

Under the old railroad bridge the Norfolk and Southern scatters the geese who have come to celebrate spring

The town of Loveland glows fresh and clean in the baptism from the clouds of heaven

How well I welcome this Buckeye Thunderstorm

To others this may seem a gloomy day, yet Eeyore, and I see something so much more

There is a special joy that comes with the sounds and color

I listen to the music upon my umbrella

This special time of worship as in recall, the words of song

I see the Lightning, I hear the rolling thunder

Then I rejoice in our God, How Great Thy Art!

Six:

Chapters

Chapters

Life is like onto a book

We live out chapters as we go along

Some written in bright colors

Others we choose to forget

Chapters of happy unions

Others of broken ties

Some chapters are love stories that scream with passion

Oh, yes Passion

Then come those dark chapters when things go wrong

The chapters of when doubt arrives

Reaching out at times to erase a line

Maybe a paragraph, or maybe a page in total

Once you have lived a chapter it becomes forever etched

No, you can't take it back

Yet, a new page turns, and you are the author

Your pen moves you beyond that wrong turn

Beyond the fork in the road

From all your yesterdays to a new day

Today

Write it with all the feelings of your heart

Do worry about spelling, you have dated Miss-Spell

Of punctuations, use not explanations' you need not explain

You have experienced the rough copy before

Your mind is wiser with experiences

Don't over-edit yourself, let the print tell your story

Tell it as it is

Move into the next chapter, be secure in your doings

Write this one with a ghost writer

One who will give you the lines, to share

One who will carry you along with a bright outlook

One who removes all the darkness you just couldn't erase

Write this one for the future

A future you never saw coming

Thank that Ghost writer

For he has given you the happy ending

When your book on earth is done you need not worry about a publisher

That is, if that Ghost writer you are working with is, the Holy Ghost

It's your book

One with no end

Seven:

Dream

Close your eyes and dream with me

Lift your thoughts away from the world

Watch for a rainbow that welcomes us a view

Listen to the breezes that tickle the leaves from the forest

Feel the warmth of the sun in a blue sky with puffy white clouds

Smell the oceans spray over the rocks

Feel the shade cast by the great mountains

Listen again as crickets announce the night

A whip-or-will calls and brings a smile

Smell the pines just beyond the woods cabin

Wet sands by the seashore welcome your naked toes

In the soft light of the moon's glow an owl calls out, “Who”

Relax in a swing hung from the large oak

Laugh at your puppy chasing a rabbit that is far too quick

Sit in a saddle ready to ride on a backwoods trail

Recline by the fire, your cat in your lap, and book in hand

Watch butterflies lift over the buttercups as bees hum along

Picnic at the edges of a stream under sycamores

Feel the crunch of the snow under your boots

The bright red cardinal sits on the fence watching for its mate

Stand in the tender touches of that light spring rain

Run through the even rows of corn ready for harvest

A doorbell rings as you hear children's voices sing, "Trick-Or-Treat"

Hold your bible by candlelight and read the Lord's prayer

Grandma's apple pie cools in a window with love baked in

The mailman leaves Valentines from someone's love proclaimed

Church bells ring out across the dawn of Easter's Sunrise service

Drive down a country road, and through the covered bridge

Watch as the eagle soars to its nest of young

Laugh a minute as the screen door slams welcoming in friends

Listen to the giggles from a newly constructed treehouse

Watch the little girl riding her bike with wind in her hair

Feel the warmth of that handmade quilt that welcomes sleep

Hold that teddy bear close, and tell it your secret

Outside with snow falling carolers sing songs of Christmas

Sit around a campfire telling old stories under the night's stars

Taste hot coco after building the best snowman ever

Feel your mother's hug that dries away tears

Balloons hang and a cake awaits, the Birthday has come

The porch swing awaits a welcome with ice-cold lemonade

The barn is holding a newborn colt finding its feet

Fences weathered in time still hold fast keeping the cows in fields

The newspaper over morning coffee, and comics bring giggles

Leaves of autumn display the colors that artist paint with love

Sit in the loft of the barn look out over the fields ready for harvest

Dads' old boots sit holding those reminders of his toils

To the nights sky fireworks lift with the joy of a new year ahead

With ripe blackberries picked cobblers soon will be a treat

Down by the pond the bullfrogs sing while dragonflies lift away

A tree filled with mistletoe will surely bring a kiss and smile

Pumpkins are ready for a Thanksgiving pie or two

Walk across that carpet of long grasses barefoot in the summer sun

There is a meadow filled with wildflowers in Gods Garden

Cattails stand at the water's edge as turtles swim for the rocks to sun

A boy has found an arrowhead with wild stories coming to life

Feel my hand in yours as now our dreams fold into the night.

Eight:

On Flat Top

The morning dew was yet showing its sparkles

Breezes from a south wind kissed across the old fence

An early Cardinal perched on a post near the gate

Its mate chirped from the maple tree

Sunlight came softly to the path above coral ridge

Now the long grasses hold cover for the young cottontail

Listening as leaves dance above the waters

Here sycamores lean close as if in prayer

Over rocks comes the singing of the river

Its flow down passes the willows and reeds

Wild geese called out lifting wings in flight

Soaring past the clouds on dawns reflections

A patch of Dutchman Britches wave with Buttercups

Wildflowers calling to the Monarch floating lazily above

There is a fragrance of blackberries wild and bees humming

Movements around wild onions, a grass snake in travel

The path rises and lifts to the lower slopes of the Scioto mountains

It is said Native American tribes walked this same earth

Higher up the air cools with the pines casting shade

Up ever higher to two lakes

One that overflows softly into the lower

Signs all around deer trails, here the whitetail come to water

Rocks on the north slope hold moss in bright green colors

High up lifting off the rocks a dead tree
holds a nest for the buzzards

Everything in nature has its place here

Even the timber rattler awaits its turn to
score

A thin trickle of water drips over the rocks
as the ferns drink

The late arrival of the snowmelt of winter
last

Winding around and up the summit is in
view

Strange it is like the mountain gave up
and just lay flat

The view is one only seen with reverence

To my feet this is Holy Ground

To my knees I pray

Words lifted beyond the horizons of blue

From this rock shelf I search for the God
of Moses

For the God of Abraham, and David

I have come not to a burning bush

I have come to offer myself lifting a voice
Talking with the creator of it all
Giving thanks
I will make camp here
I will serve coffee hot and black
I will ask God to join me
I am here to have coffee with the Lord

Nine:

Rainbow

Color me a rainbow with love

Give me a coat of color like Joseph

Splash on a bit of green for growth

Yellow sunshine for warmth

Red for a smile from the heart

Brown for the soil from which God made us

Brush on white for cleanliness

A dab of silver for wisdom

Blue for the waters of Baptism

Touches of pink for tenderness

Lastly paint the gold of heaven that awaits

Those black sins have been forgiven

Color me, a child of God.

Ten:

Home

Come Home

Down that old road

Past the church on the corner

Down on the right side

Past the mailbox

There it stood

The old house as I recalled

The yard where we played ball

The horseshoe pit ready

The clothesline filled on wash day

The back porch where we stood on rainy days

The kitchen door that was never locked

Home cooking lifting in the air

That table that held us all

Home was this and so much more

It was a place of growing

Finding ourselves in life

The phone that was once on a party line

The neighbors we knew everyone

A place to celebrate the seasons and holidays

Here we would listen to one of dad's stories

Here we would create art from broken crayons

Here my brother looked to the heavens from his first telescope

Here my sister played a piano

Here another brother used his hands on making a car go faster

Here where I left home at too young to see the world

Here where our baby brother too would follow

Come Home

One can never come back home

We were the birds of the nest

We took to our wings

We moved with the winds

Some took root not far from that homestead

Some just across the river

My sister for a while just across the street

My little brother settled a bit more south

Me well it seemed I never could settle

Just here for a spell, then somewhere else

Come home

It echoed in my mind at times

The pictures of home etched in my mind

All too short it is gone

The old road gone

No house remains

The church gone

Mom and dad too

There is a treasure chest of memories

They come into the night at times
My old self young again
All the folks we knew there at times
Then I awake
Come home
Well, I will
I will come home again
But not in these horizons
My home is beyond the stars
Beyond the world
I will come home to rest
Rest with that circle that won't be broken
Till then I have a few things to do
I will follow my God as he directs
I will stand up for Jesus
I will pray for those in need and give a helping hand
I will tell the greatest story ever told
Then when the time comes, and he calls

I will

Come home

Eleven:

Cowboy Christmas Eve

Cowboy Christmas Eve

Off the trail towards a place called home
To be around folks one loves
Too long gone with dreams that fail
Married to a horse and old dog
Riding ranges of endless land
Years have passed all too quickly
Winter can be bitter with its breath
Campfires fight but lose to keep one warm
The last few miles come with the ringing of bells
The church in celebration of Christmas
Sitting the saddle now with a quicken pace
To join with mom and dad
Music lifts over the snow

Sweet songs of the birth of Jesus

Away in a manger comes to him with tears

Folks turn and look with smiles

The desperado came home

Moving down the aisle mom cries in welcome

Dad pulls him in with a hug

Tonight, he will sleep under a warm quilt

He will reflect on new tomorrows

Old yesterday's lay broken in a troubled mind

He is down to four round gold coins

And this is his offering to God

No matter he knows the love of money makes a fool

Holding on to a worn song book he sings

Silent Night, with a voice just above a whisper

Standing there he feels someone move to his side

Her voice rings like an angel

It is Holly, the girl he left behind

She smiles as if it were yesterday when they were in their youth

He touches her hand lightly

She takes it with a warm squeeze

Maybe it is not too late

Maybe his travels have brought him where he needs to be

He closes his eyes to lift a silent prayer

When he opens again everything is gone

The Church, mom, dad, and Holly

He is outside in the cold snow of winter

It is Christmas Eve

He packs up all his shabby belongings and rides out

Over the crest of the mountains down towards home

Stars break through the darkness as he pushes on

Riding now with purpose

Riding with hope

He will be home come Christmas morning

His prayer lifted that as moonlight fell over the trail

In the late hours long past midnight he sees the light

The candle in the window flickered

This Christmas Eve has brought him home

Then a voice came with the winds

As he listened to God

"Ascribe to the Lord of families of the peoples, ascribe to the Lord glory and strength."

He entered his home with rejoicing and celebration

Warm tears around the fire of reunion

Mom read the story of Christ and his birth

They prayed together and slept the sleep of peace

He awoke as the snow had lifted away

Then to the little church to welcome in Christmas

Then just as in his trail dream, Holly, held to his hand

The cowboy was home.

Just a cowboy Christmas Eve to remember

It is now my prayer that all the cowboys make it home

To give up old dreams and find new trails

To find the love of God and family

To celebrate the wonders

Twelve:

Golden Treasure

Sitting by the fire at night

Watching the flickers and sparks

Smoke lifts like prayers up and out of sight

Here with an old dog by one side

A horse tied at rest

A cowboy looks beyond himself

Lays his head on the saddle for a pillow

Looking up to the stars that spread full in the horizons

That worn saddlebag holds his treasures in life

A letter from home faded with time

The pocket watch given by a father long ago

The harmonica that knows the old gospel songs

Twenty-two dollars and thirty-six cents

A bar of soap in a handkerchief

A ribbon from the hair of a lady once loved

A small pencil sharpened by his trail knife

Paper two pages folded into an envelope awaiting words

A can of beans and one of peaches

Two books one of poems, and the other a bible

Some trail clothes and a poncho

Traveling as always, no extras

God supplies what is needed

Lifting his prayer, he says the same prayer every night

The one Jesus gave to his disciples

Our father he prays and lays now to rest

The lone cry lifts from the coyotes

It is an exchange of shared geography

One might wonder about sleeping in the wild

Yet, the cowboy would tell you he sleeps in the hand of God

His boots covered in the dust of the earth

He might report it is of the same of which God made man

Turning the pages in his bible as he lays by firelight to read

Tonight, it is a story from Isaiah that brings comfort

He touches a faded rose before closing the holy pages

A rose that even now brings tears

There is a story within but kept as a treasure to himself

Old dog lays close as now the embers glow

The moon opens up sending down its reflection

The cowboy sleeps with an ear to the earth and one to God

Never knowing what might awaken him

Tomorrow's trial will take him across the high mountains

On the other side two more days and home

Seems time for the parodical to return

No gold found, no rainbows yielding

Just one old soul finding the values of life are not of this earth

Finding favor and salvation from Jesus in a tent meeting in Santa Fe

This is his golden treasure now

Going home to share it freely

Thirteen:

Don't Pass Me By

Did You pass me by?

Looking the other way?

Your life too busy to stop

Afraid to speak

It's OK I am used to this world

One growing colder than the snow

So much hate and lack of love it seems

Some say my name at times, but don't know me

Others curse me for who I am

I am not asking for things of this world

I am giving

I am offering what you cannot get otherwise

Not money

Not fame

Just life and salvation

Jesus

Fourteen:

Dreams

Dreams

The Magic of The Mind
They Come to us All
Rich, Poor, Young, Old
A Vision of something Beyond
The Sweet Sleep
A Vision of Goodness
That Soft Touch we almost feel
Smiles found in the Heart
Dreams of Life
Birthday Dreams
Valentines Dreams
Christmas Dreams
Dreams of Tomorrows
Dreams of Hope
Dreams to make us Better
Dreams of Love
Dreams of Sharing
Hold fast to your Dreams
Don't let the world hold you back
See the Colors
The Beauty

The Joy
Remember old Dreams
Plant Seeds of New
Dream with a Prayer
Let go of Fear
Embrace the Darkness with Dreams
These are the gifts of the Angels
Given to the Magic of the Mind

Fifteen:
Good Night

End of the Day

A good horse first to get food, and rest

The old dog, well him too

As for me

Time to head to the bunkhouse

Kick the dust off my boots

Beans and taters, and coffee black

Sit back in a tub of water by the open fire

Dry off and read a little from the good book

God knows what I need

Say my prayers

Hope to sleep till the sun rises

Good night from this end of the rope

Sixteen:

Treasures

Found treasures

It was an arrowhead

I put it in a cigar box

Then added a four leafed clover

A buffalo Nickle

Then a stamp from Ireland

A Valentine from somebody I didn't know

Then a two-dollar bill

An I.O.U. to God

That ring that turned my finger green

Two rocks smooth from the creek

A baseball card of someone nobody knows

From the monopoly game a "Get out of Jail Free" card

The skate key that belonged to my sister

Two marbles, a steel shooter, and a cat-eye

The Timex watch that didn't keep on ticking

Swiss Army knife with a broken big blade

Plastic army man

Two checkers one black, one red

Ticket stub to a baseball game that got rained out

Assorted Cracker Jack toys (The good ones)

A Roy Rogers cap pistol

Also, a water gun that leaks a little

My best yo-yo ever

The kazoo that got me in trouble at school

Popsicle stick stained orange

A rubber clown nose

The golf ball found in the pond

Red and white whistle with a ball inside

Three for a quarter picture of myself

Bazooka Bubble Gum, unopened

Bottle cap from a Royal Crown Cola

Oh, such were the treasures of my youth

Today I wonder what children will save.

Will they wish upon the first star of night?

Read with excitement about some, Never, Never, Land?

Will lightning bugs bring them a lantern that flickers?

Does anyone look for four leafed clovers?

Do kids play pick up sticks anymore?

Do kids ride bikes with playing cards flapping in the spokes?

Will they make a homemade kite?

Those soapbox cars are they lost to history?

One might tell when life has been lived in the "Good Old Days" when the things of their youth are just lost to the world that once was.

Seventeen:

Gethsemane

Gethsemane
What was it to Jesus?
He knew what he was called to do
He knew what lay ahead
He knew his betrayer
He knew it was his time
He knew it
The Garden of Gethsemane
It was here he prayed
His prayers were for strength
How great was his sorrow?
Angels came to be with him
Angels while his disciples lay asleep
Jesus lifted his voice
His time was fading like the night
He knew, oh how he knew

Gethsemane
He prayed that the cup might pass
That what was ahead
Then he prayed
“Thy will be done,” words to his father
At Gethsemane he awoke the disciples
Then he spoke
“Behold the hour is at hand,
And the son of man is betrayed
Into the hands of Sinners”
Here at Gethsemane, he spoke
“Rise, let us be going.
See, my betrayer is at hand”
Judas came with a kiss
He spoke, “Hail Master” and kissed him
Judas came with a crowd
A crowd with swords and clubs
The chief priest and elders came
They seized him at Gethsemane

Here while his prayer lifted yet warm to the heavens

He was taken away from Gethsemane

Gethsemane in my youth was the name of my church

It was a long name for me with too many letters

I never understood early on what it was all about

It was a church with hard wood benches

Here preachers lifted words in prayer too

Words of prayer from my Gethsemane

Then came understanding

Then came my tears

Then I too prayed at Gethsemane

There was no Judas, but Christ was there

He lifted me up from those hard benches

I walked down the aisle and accepted him as savior

I was baptized at Gethsemane

I had a long way to go in a Christian life

It was at an early age I left my Gethsemane

I traveled the world and went to war

I traveled this country too looking for rainbows

I was tested and failed many times

But he forgave me anyway

While I was gone my Gethsemane was taken down

The same church of my youth gone

One the very same street as my home, gone too

There remain just memories

Memories of praying the night I found Jesus

Memories of baptism

Memories of those hard benches that I would love to sit upon again

Jesus never went back to Gethsemane

He was tried with lies

He was condemned to a cross

He suffered giving of his blood

He lay in a tomb

Then, he arose

Jesus followed the will of his father

Each year upon this week I lift prayers

Prayers for a Jesus, a king with a crown of thorns

Prayers for the man who prayed at Gethsemane

Prayers to follow the will of my God

We have both been to our Gethsemanes, just a world apart

His from a garden outside Jerusalem

Mine from a little church in Kentucky

Yet we were both touched by the hand of God

Eighteen:

Going Home

Going Home

I have gone home a thousand times

Yet never arrived

I took a wrong turn

A bend in the road

There was a detour

Then came a storm

Darkness too

I was always going home

Something happened, something got in the way

Time turned to days

Days to weeks, and weeks to months, and before long years

Winds of life blew me like a tumbling weed it seems

Across endless sands I traveled

Over hills and down to the low valleys

There was the flood and a river I could not cross

Then came the winter cold, Ice, snow, and frozen time

I was always going home

Could almost see the town's lights

Could feel the closeness

Old voices I longed to hear

Yet came another setback, maybe next year

Then that year passed, and another one too

A lifetime of traveling and another mile or two

I was always going home

But never made my way

Some tell me it is no longer there
No longer will I see those faces
My tears of sorrow, I cry
Too many were my burdens in life
That kept me so far away
Almost made it, but never did

I was always going home
Now I travel no more
Home is on another shore
The house of home it no longer stands
Yet my memories all I recall
Tonight, I will dream again
The way I always do
Maybe tonight, I will make it home
If not,
I was always going home

Nineteen:

Church Bell Rang

The grey and white sky covered day
Winds cold with snow soon to arrive
She sat with a blue coat just watching
The open fire lifting sparks to the air
The smell of wood smoke her perfume
There by her side a little brown dog
Her hand folded around a letter
Her love had gone to war
The words were of his not returning
Lost on some far away shore
Tears of loss creased her face
The little dog moved closer, offering love
The letter tossed to the flame
The hour passed and then another
The two huddled close, she and her dog
Snow began to fall

White and pure over the fields it came

Colder now another log to the fire

Smoke lifting like a prayer through the falling snow

Her dog now sat upon her lap

She held it to her heart

Off, down in the village a church bell rang

But she sat with her God and dog

A prayer of thanksgiving lifted

One for their time together and memories made

There in the twilight she prayed, her knees in the snow

Prayed for peace and an end to another war

Prayed for others too, those not coming home

Asking that they might be lifted up to heaven's door

As snow deepened, she stood and cast a look to the heavens

God must have seen her pain and sorrow

As there in the dead of wind stood her with a rose

A rose from heaven sent

Somehow, someway, her dog lay it at her feet

A blessing no one could believe

She picked up her little dog

And held tight to the rose

Her in her blue coat, little brown dog, and a rose.

That was the winter before spring

Then she gave birth to a son

And love returned to her heart, and home

And she was blessed with a garden filled with roses

And three new puppies

And the church bells rang

Twenty:

The Hand and the Pencil

Hands Reach Out with A Pencil

Scratching marks across endless pages
Words crashing to others
Books and binders hold thousands
Some God gives wings to
He the master of subjects
In his call I hold the pencil
I push on to another page
Another sheet fills with thoughts
Sometimes a parable
Sometimes a prayer
Sometimes just words to color tomorrow
Darkness even has a purpose to my God
Not a place to hide in the shadows

A place to think beyond, with a prayer through the clouds

Some words fall like flowers of his beauty

Some to songs to sing

I am the holder of the pencil

God is the hand that moves the words

Twenty-One:

He Had a Dream

He Had a Dream

Never again will he dream

But I remember as tears stream

A man who stood in the shadows of God

Who walked this earth where others feared to trod?

A man of black with a dream for us all

But I remember as tears stream

A man who stood in the shadows of God

Who walked this earth where others feared to trod?

A man of black with a dream for us all

Sad it was in Memphis he had to fall

But he left us all with a spirit of light

A message did not end that dreadful night

Now we honor him for his vision to see

What from a dream could really be?

I was stationed at the Naval Air Technical Training Center located just outside Memphis the night of the shooting of Martin Luther King Jr. April 4th, 1968, I still feel the shock and horror of the events at the Lorain Motel and a great since of loss for a disciple of equality and peace. I however rejoice in that the "Dream Lives On" and now, so we pick up the cross. Each year I lift a prayer to honor the man and the God, he served.

Twenty-Two:

Maybe

Help
The cry from problems
Maybe a prayer to lift
Maybe a loss of faith
Maybe

Help me Lord
There that is better
I may not have an answer right away
But it's coming
Maybe

Maybe God must stop to giggle
My request is not from being lazy
It is because I lack understanding
He might have to think it over
Maybe

I recall prayers as a child
The one for a pony
No, I never got a pony
I was lacking in faith
Maybe

Now that I think of it
He gave me a horse
Many years later
Now I am too old to ride
Maybe

I am not sure why I needed a pony
I think it was to show off
That is a sin
That is why the pony never came
Maybe

Help me Lord

To become wiser in this life
To use prayer the right way
To pray with a greater faith
To pray for needs not wants

P.S. thanks for not sending the pony

Twenty-Three:

Hold Me

Hold me
Let me feel your love
Let me feel your devotion
Let me feel your faith
Hold me when you are troubled
Hold me when you find tears
Hold me when you just need me
Be the heart filled with my love
Be the heart that shares this light
Be the heart that warms others
Walk with me through the darkness
Walk with me through all your days
Walk with me that others may see
Call me with your whispers
Call me with hope
Call me with faith

Work with me as called
Work with me in this world
Work with me freely
Pray with me in all things
Pray for others in their needs
Pray with powers within
Reflect me to others
Reflect me in all things
Reflect me to this world
Hold me yes
Hold me close
Hold me always
Love me as I love you
Love me in all things
Love me for I first loved you
Hold me
Jesus

Twenty-Four:

How Many More

How many Memorial Days do we celebrate?
A lifetime of tears fills the soil in memory
Those who gave it all will give no more
Many forgotten markers lost to the earth
Battles for peace seem so odd to be printed in the same ink, within the same sentence.
The bible the most holy book says it in John 15:13
And today we burn with tears at the memory of those
Those lost through the ages
Those who of now, taps are played
I count names I have known that touched my life
Those that will see never another day in these horizons
Jesus gave his life for our salvation and in, so we celebrate, Easter
Others gave their lives, in some war for peace and in, so we celebrate Memorial Day

Memorial Day is not a day to worship a sale in some store
It is not a day for burgers and hot dogs
It is not a day just to celebrate a day away from our labors
A day to fill the night air with fireworks and wine
It is a day to recall a loss in prayer and memory
It is a day to honor those who gave us this thing called freedom
That same freedom being fought for in other lands
The same blood given to the soil of what we call God's good earth
If you are touched by one name
One soul that has lifted away in this cause
You must celebrate that memory with tears and prayers
Go to the beaches
Go to the picnics
Go on and celebrate freedom
Go on and recall, however, how it was paid for
Where have all the young men gone?
Where too the women in arms
Where will tomorrow's flowers grow

Those planted in the soils of peace
War and Peace
Love and hate
Color the mind with rainbows or darkness
Oh, that we could reach out to truly, love our enemies
I thank those who try
I thank those who die in the process
I shed my tears that clouds the ink to the page
The ink of mankind written in the blood of a memory
Memorial Day, how many more do we celebrate?

Twenty-Five:
I Don't Hear Him Anymore

I Don't hear him anymore

"It was a long time ago"

"I really don't recall"

"Maybe I cried that day"

"I felt something inside"

"Deep inside in my mind and soul"

"He spoke to me then"

"I don't hear him anymore"

"It may have been part of the music"

"Maybe the words too"

"I don't hear him anymore"

"Not in this world"

"Not at this time"

"My feet would not move that day"

"I stood holding to an old wooden bench"

"They sang just as I am"

"I was almost persuaded"

"Almost"

"I don't hear him anymore"

"Sometimes I think about it"

"Sometimes"

"Maybe I'll go back someday"

"Maybe I'll listen to the music"

"Maybe the word"

"I wonder if my feet could move"

"If I would let go of the old wooden bench"

"I wonder if I'll still be always, just as I am"

"Maybe if I listen very hard"

"Maybe I could be Persuaded"

"Maybe"

These could be the words of many in this life who heard the voice and did not follow the call. Stumbling through life always looking and never finding. Sometimes a faint voice lingers in recall. The shadows of dreams become lost in the night. This world will never give anything to take to a beyond. The only beyond this world is through Jesus. In death the old wooden bench will be empty of the hand that griped it. Will it be the epitaph in words etched to a stone, "Here I lay, just as I am."

The voice is still there, the words spoken too, you have only to just listen.

Twenty-Six:

Tall Mountain Shadow

I have been a shadow on a tall mountain

In the early light of dawn, I arose and cast my view from whence I came

My shadow fell long to the path that brought me to this summit

It was my past that was shadowed in the dawn of day

Here I stood looking over the rocks and hard places I had walked

The wrong turns by not looking more forward

Those footsteps that fell on misguided soil

Yet for the grace of God Himself I made the journey

I slept in the light of the moon's glow and rested in those soft shadows

The dawn in passing as my shadow moves about

From that path of yesterday to now

By the noon hours the shadow lays at my feet just a small circle

A circle of me as I am in the now

It is not looking back but realizing the rewards of becoming a new me

The sky is clear with the eagle in flight delivering a message of peace

So comes the hunger and thirsting of the body I take in the fruits of the harvest and drink of the cup of knowledge

As this now passes; comes my shadow cast to the path on the unopened side of the mountain

Down through the trees capturing the fair light of an afternoon sun

My shadow falls deeply, growing longer to what is yet to be

With eyes looking beyond the shadows fades to a valley never walked

As twilight unfolds my thoughts find me
somewhere in those shadows on the path
not yet traveled

This is the time of preparation of
tomorrow as prayers are lifted to my God
who knows all my shadows

Stars twinkle in the horizons each with a
light of no shadow to cast just in a darken
space to be viewed by mankind

How lovely they look as this world spins
past them

They, a gate to something beyond to the
maker of it all

It is a realization like onto Moses at the
burning bush, on another mountain that
God spoke

He speaks here too, words whispered in
the winds that flow over this mountain
top

Words of direction of life for me, and my
shadow ahead

Lifting prayers of thanks and understanding I will rest in his hands on this lofty place

Dawn will come and of that light I will move where the light is directed

Over the paths towards the valley and will share my shadow with others

We will unite in the treasures of a spirit from whom our shadows are reflected

That shadow of our Lord, Jesus Christ

Mountains may crumble, shadows fall, but I have been on high with the Holy One and seen into myself to the soul that has been collected in the calling of one from a cross, a shadow that was cast to the blood shed on the ground, from another hill.

Twenty-Seven:

I Stand In The Shadow

The pen moved lightly
Floating just above the page
Then the winds of my mind called to it
Across the blank spaces it kissed the page
Words placed in a line
Each talking in the voice of ink
Down came the flow like blood to the page
Part of myself became its beating heart
As the page filled it exposed me
The hand that held the pen began to shake
The confession lay darken
Tears joined the ink as it washed down the page
Traces of failure leaked on, word upon word

My room grew dark with the storm from within

Like thunder the paper screamed

Lightning flashed from my candle

Rain of tears splashed as the confession grew

Many pages followed as the confession became a book

The book lay upon my desk closed as I prayed

Words whispered to my God

I asked for forgiveness so underserved

My sins so many

Then upon my shoulder I felt the hand of Jesus

My pen lay empty of its ink

My voice a whisper

My shattered life once so hopeless

Now had peace

I held the book of confession up and he touched it

The pages lay pure and white

Not a word remained within

I was forgiven of all my sins

On the cover there lay one drop of his blood

That drop washed away all the darkness from within

The storm passed over

As the glow of God was cast all around

And in this I stand in the shadow of Jesus

Twenty-Eight:

It Is For You, I Do It All

Sometimes I am lost

Can't see at all

Sometimes I stumble

Sometimes I fall

But even if I have to crawl

It is for you, I do it all

Darkness and shadows around me may be cast

An unholy angel tries to void me from my tasks

Old bones now move with pain of age

Your call however calls me to another page

Over the mountains high or the deeper valleys trod

It is for you, I do it all, for you, my God

Tears I cry at times over sin

You lift me up, forgiven again

It is with that pen you have me to write

Thoughts you bring from the darkness to light

It is your hand that moves the ink, as I let it fall

It is for you, I do it all

Now to those who have lost their sight

To a page of braille, you it is passed on in the night

And of those who cannot hear

Words are printed to strengthen when lost in fear

A path that was lost, through prayer I saw

It is for you, I do it all

In those times in the darkest of nights

I cannot hear, and have lost my sight

I hold to you most when at your test

To be like Christ and reflect my best

You are the light that shines even as fog might fall

It is for you, I do it all

Someday my task with surely end

But I will live on, and meet you then

You my father and I your adoption from sin

It is for you, I do it all, and will again, and again to the end

"You shall not curse the deaf or put a stumbling block before the blind, but you shall fear your God: I am the Lord."

Words from Leviticus 19-14 this is the challenge I face

To open the ears, and eyes to Gods' love and grace

It is of God that all might see and hear

Help me Lord, to be your servant always near

Being old and tired you move me yet at your call

It is for you, I do it all

Twenty-Nine:

John Doe

One lost moment
Time mattered not
Tears fell
Wet and warm
Why
Words lost no answer
He lay lifeless
In the dust he lay
Screams only cried from within
We never knew
He never expressed himself
Hands folded around the needle
That last rush took him away
The pain too much
A child of the streets he became
His name unknown

They will tag him, John Doe
He will become just a number
Once a mother's son
For this one I prayed
I prayed yet he never knew me
I prayed for his soul
I prayed for peace within
One he never had
One drug of mankind too strong
An overdose they said
How could I have known
How could I help
The answer is in now Gods hand
A man that fought for the peace of this country
But lost that peace within
The war for him never ended
The battles came home
They walked the streets of his mind

Haunted day and night

The noise too much

That flash in the mind too bright

The cries always hearing

Life had no value, no worth, no hope, no reason

People walk by and turn their faces away

Never to see a fallen life

He may have known them once

Played sports in school

Broke bread together

But they don't want to know

Don't want to see

No prayers lifted here

The body placed in a bag like trash

That is what this world sees

A junkie they may think

Maybe so

But there was a person before this

A face that once had a real smile

A voice that sang music

But came the war

A war that took a mind

A war that took him to become another number

A number in a record book as the ink fades

Who will remember this day?

The day of ending

Who

In his pocket only one remembrance

A purple heart

Faded and dirty

Have mercy Oh, God

A-Men

John Doe and a Purple heart

Thirty:

Life Fell Into Me On Easter

Life fell into me on Easter
A day of celebration of Jesus
A day of hope for the world
A day for remembrance of a promise given
A day of song and cheers
Halleluiah
Yes, after the blood was spilled
The body broke
The cup taken
The bread broken
Life fell into me on Easter
Halleluiah
A-Men

Thirty-One:

Lullaby of The Oak Tree

Lullaby of the Oak Tree

Back in the hot days of summer

When childhood was free

One might lay under the shade of the oak

There is a fragrance from those clovers in which we rested

The soft coolness itself was welcome

Most times we might lay and just peak at the sky

Through the leaves little splashes of sunlight came

Sparkles leaving designs in the shade

We might lay looking at the clouds in change

Each one folded and unfolded into pictures of the mind

Then came the breezes of the Kentucky air

Moving the leaves one way then another

The fluttering of each became a song

Notes we listen to with eyes closed

A lullaby it seemed

So, it is today that I recall that lullaby of the oak tree

Thirty-Two:

Magic Star Dust

Magic Star Dust
Looking up at the night sky
Looking to the right side of the moon
Left past the Milky-Way
That is where the magic star dust lies
It comes from breezes of the outer space winds
Blows across the universe
Then at just the right time falls into the minds of humans
We the people of the earth
We breath in the magic dust
It changes us into something different
Magic carpets lift us
We ride to strange lands
We experience new things never before thought of

Like Peter Pan we pass over the Never-
Never-Lands

We sail waters in Neptune's hand

Stepping into a time machine we view
history firsthand

From great rockets we soar across very
distant skies to the tomorrows

Our eyes see all the colors of life swirling
around a forest in the enchanted forest

We communicate with giants and fairies

We are touched by a happiness displayed

Then moved by sorrows overcome

Dancing to the music of Angels we drift in
the ballroom of love

Climbing the mountains, we sit with the
eagles

Then the rainforest opens to all its
wonders

We taste the teas of the orient

The poems tickle us with understanding

We sleep in dreams of lullaby's that whisper peace

Then when it is time

We awake with ourselves in the library

The books have brought us all this and more

Covers, titles, pages, and ink have offered us everything

We only need to reach out

Touch and feel

Thirty-Three:

My Garden Tree

My Garden Tree

There is a tree in my garden
It's not so very tall
And slightly shades the moonlight
From the ground where it might fall

A warm breeze passes gently through
As the limbs whisper a call
It's the holy breath of heaven
God gives freely to us all

There is a tree in my garden
Where I go to pray
As even night birds listen
For the voice my Lord, what he will say

Like angels all around me
Leaves flicker in twilight of day
Singing songs of his returning
Time now, Jesus is on his way

There is a tree in my garden
There was one at Calvary too
My Saviors blood was shed up on it
This with love for me and you

The wood it held the weight
Of Gods' only begotten son
For six hours in the time of man
The tree and he were one

Now, there is no tree at Calvary
Nor one in my garden man can see
It's with my faith; in the believing
A tree of life grows for all eternity

Do you have a tree in your garden?

This is not just a vision for me

I have a tree in my garden

It's Jesus, the tree of life

That is the tree I see

This old poem was cast within the pages of my bible after I scratched it out back in Louisville, Kentucky, 1963 and yet it fits today maybe, a world looking to the forest all around that may only need to see but one tree. I pray you take up the seed and plant it in your heart and watch it grow as the tree in your garden.

Thirty-Four:

No Longer Do I Sail The Seas

No longer do I sail the seas

Neptune and I have called a truce

He and the maidens of the waters and I

We trade not storms anymore

The winds blow on the Youngman's sails

Those lofty dreams of adventure less calling

Standing on a sandy shore I watch the seabirds play

The old lighthouse yet cast its beam through a darken night

There is peace ashore as starfish lay in the sand

Old driftwood lays awaiting a writer's words

Sandcastles now I see till the tides come

Age has calmed me to view red skies of night

Tis true a sailors', delight
Just a shack upon a distant shore
That's all I need, nothing more
To live with the breezes that softly blow
This and a unclouded day
Sun to cast a warmer glow
Rest in peace as the waters flow
Old come age too late I learn
Treasures of life are not at rainbow end
They are here to view as our good God does send
I might stand and recall with a smile
The seas of the world only brought me home
Home where my feet belong
Those wayward days that all went wrong
An angle came in prayers to set me free
Now the world may have that restless sea
I await another horizon one found beyond these shores

Tis now I scribe with pen and ink

Come join me; let me tell the tale that you may hear

The treasures of God I hold so dear

Jesus is the ship I sail over yonder shores

Come along and take in the view

Pray with me as I pray with you

Thirty-Five:

Soft Sweet Midnight

Sweet soft midnight awakens me

Calling me from yesterday last moments

Opening now my eyes to a new day

The very early birth before a light of dawn

As the moon slides across the silent horizon

I listen for my God

Lifting prayers to his house

Prayers for so many in need

Each one addressed to his attention

Lives in the balance lingering

Lives that have moved beyond this earthly road

Prayers for those fallen looking and listening to a dark angel

Words spoken of a war for freedom

Homes broken as lives shatter into numbers called ended

Words of hope lifted to the hopeless

Praying for the homeless, those souls without direction

Praying for those that hear not and see not

Praying for those that need of food, clothing, medicines, and a helping hand of friendship

Praying for those who are looking to death as an answer to their pain and sufferings

Those that have lost hope in this new day

Praying for those who lean on drugs and alcohol as an answer

Praying for the two hearts broken from a marriage bond slipping

Praying again and again for those that face each day alone

Praying for family the blood ties that they are blessed in love

Praying for family that are not of my blood but of a brotherhood of Jesus

Praying now for myself

Praying to be used by the hand of God himself

To be walking closer to Jesus, ever closer

Praying for forgiveness in my moments of failure

Open my heart and mind to such a world I pray

Open my life to a purpose in heavens call

I pray for the church that it may open doors to the needs of the soul

Praying for that house of God that prays with convictions

Praying for the testimonies that open hearts that hear

Praying for those of the pulpits to use that holy ground in God's name, and to welcome the spirt into the assembly

Praying for the music that lifts to the heavens, words of song in worship, that joyful noise that calls to each life with each note

Praying ever to be in the shadow of God holding away the door of the evil one

Praying for those lives known to me, introduced I as friends

Praying for those yet to be known that we might share a common bond

Praying for that child that is born to this world that it may know my God and follow in his ways

Praying for the congregations who gather in worship that the blessing may be many, and their lives a reflection unto Jesus beyond that service and into their lives.

Praying for those who with tears that fall in their lives the ones that get up and give a deeper service.

Praying for those who paint the colors of life that their rainbows bless the eye of the beholder

Praying for the words given by the poets
that they bring an awaking

Praying for the songs that sing with the
fullness of love

Praying for those the workers of this
world that they know that all lives matter

Praying for the races of mankind that
harmony might be warmly felt, and hate
washed away

Praying with thankfulness for all the
blessings of my life

Praying to shut my mouth from all
grumbling and open it to praise

Praying for the heart united with me in
my efforts to serve

Praying to also be a helping hand to that
my helpmate

Now with all these prayers lifted I listen to
hear what my God might say

Listening for a voice clearly be it bold or
still small

Listening with my mind, heart, soul and with a humble bow to his holy voice.

He may not speak a word in return or maybe he will just direct me as he wills but I will listen.

This midnight has passed with prayers many lifted

This day as clouds gather on the horizons, I will still walk in the light of the greater light that blinded Saul to become Paul

This day when the bible calls out with words to be studied, and a message understood for the purpose of sharing the good news within

The A-Men lifted now will become the start of another prayer to come that I might listen ever closer to what my God may have to say

I pray that A-Men opens the doors that God may know my heart.

Yes, and the heart of all who pray as such

A-Men

That soft midnight has now passed, and prayers lifted to this new day may our God talk to the hearts of all mankind throughout the hours ahead wherever we go and that which we do be it for him we walk

Thirty-Six:

The Jesus I Never Knew

The Jesus I never knew
I never saw him in Bethlehem
I never viewed him with the shepherds
I never saw the gifts from the three kings
I never heard him in the temple as a boy
I never saw him walk on water
I wasn't there with the twelve
I never heard his words in parables
I wasn't there when he prayed at Gethsemane
I wasn't there when they cried, "Crucify Him"
I wasn't there when he was nailed to a cross
I wasn't there when they placed him in a tomb
I wasn't there when he arose

I wasn't there then

I am there now

I found salvation

I found truth in all he did

I found myself in Jesus

Yes, there is a Jesus I never knew, but there is one I now do

He is Alive!

Thirty-Seven:

The Train Comes No More

The train comes no more

No Hobos, no Midnight Gamblers

The rails rust in a silent steel death

Lost to nature's grip

It must have been a long black train

The clatter of wheels no more

Smoke has cleared the horizons

The sound of a whistle that old Hank once sang

Maybe it was a train of Jonny that had rich folks eating in fancy dining car, probably drinking coffee, and smoking long cigars

Maybe it was a train that carried men to war

Men that never came home

That train comes no more

The station is gone as are the travelers

Jessie James has put away his evil ways

It might have been that midnight train to Georgia

Maybe the one of old Casey Jones

Old spikes that held the rails holding now in rust and rot

Beside the track lost coal lays never to warm the cold

Boxcar Willie has retired

This train gone lost in time

Hurston McCoy may have been such an engineer

Riding the rails behind the old Union Terminal

Now he too is retired

What becomes of the rails that are empty?

They lay as markers like long tombstones

No words etched of their birth or death

The train comes no more

Boxcars now on other rails
Tankers too
Dinning cars filled with ghost
The old conductors checking tickets in some lost dream
No one stand with suitcases
No goodbye kisses shared
No greetings for home comings
The rails have their stories
Words lost in time never to be told
The rails over bridges sag with age
Time has passed them by
Rails that were dreams have turned to rust
Old stories may be yet told
Yet the real thing is
The train comes no more

Thirty-Eight:

The Universe

The Universe

Just looking out to the night

Far past the vision of this Earth

Beyond the Moon

Beyond the Milky Way

Even beyond the Blackhole

To what is out there

The further beyond

Stars, Planets, Sun, Moons, that greater beyond

From our Mother Earth, we reach out with eyes in those skies

Eyes that travel sending back visions of the beyond

We have viewed the dark side of the Moon

We have sent men to walk there upon

We have sent eyes beyond for knowledge

What is our greater gain?

Those eyes that search the horizons of horizons

What lies beyond the shadows?

Words beyond that may have lived and died

Our own world that swirls around the great Universe

Is it coming to its doom?

Will it end at the hands that poison the air, water, and the soil itself?

Or maybe, God himself will step in again

The master that placed it all into a creation

Will this son of his Jesus return as foretold?

Will we be lifted to a higher horizon yet?

Our eyes might view the outer limits

Far beyond this Universe

But it is the very soul of man that God is reaching to

That connection with the hand that put it all in place

I might look beyond, yet I must also look within

To the self that already knows what is out there

To make ready my trip from this earth to a far greater place

I believe that the longest living documents recorded it

I believe that a greater love has given us a ticket to the beyond

Beyond the hate of this world

The sickness, the death of the body.

I believe our souls will unite with others that have that same belief

Some dry bones may lay deep in the soil of this earth, but the souls that believe will live on

This I believe

I believe on Jesus Christ as my Savior

I believe I don't even need to see beyond, to know what is already evident, my heart is changed, my mind is clear, and my soul is ready.

I believe in the life of Jesus, the son of God, and have faith in a life beyond a spinning earth in a cycle around this thing called Universe.

I will tell the old story over and over and pray that you are ready for your ticket too.

Thirty-Nine:

Wisdom of Youth

What Happened?

There is wisdom in youth

Wisdom lost as we grow older

Those happy faces change

Why?

Did they learn to dislike?

Did they learn to hate?

Did they find something too different from themselves?

Who teaches such things?

Does it start at home?

Does it come from school?

Does it come all at once, or a little at a time?

Why can't the world see things from the eyes of youth?

What Happened?

Is this as it should be?

Do we fold into something of darkness?
Does this grow deeper with age?
Oh, where is the smiles of youth?
Where is the happiness?
Where is the sharing together?
What happened?
Did this all start in a garden in the bible?
God Knows
Do You?

Forty:

Wet Prayers

Wet Prayers

There are times when we are moved to tears

When God reveals himself to us over our sins

Other times when we lose a loved one, or friend

Then there are times we are overcome by this world

We see the evil now called good

Tears and prayers flow together

Realization tears find us when we cannot turn our backs

At an alter call we find tears

Wet prayers, a moment with God in weeping

It seems to leave us somehow closer

I am not ashamed to cry for then I feel changed

That flood of tears is talking for my heart

Talking in an exchange, man with God

Dry prayers, words lifted like a weather report

Like a rehearsed speech

Hands folded but words less felt given to ears not of God

Feel what you say, give conviction in your words, cry from within

Pray with faith in the name of Jesus

Pray deep from within

Pray with tears to him most holy

Praying, wet prayers.

Hello God, it's me again, praying for this world

Praying with sorrow of how we have treated what you created

Praying for those who won't pray for themselves

Praying for lives in endless wars

Praying for minds drifting seeing only darkness

Praying for so many in pain and sickness

Praying for a way to be of service while on this earth

Praying for family, blood of blood

Praying for babies yet unborn that might be cast aside

Praying for neighbors in whatever needs be addressed

Praying for love, the tenderness of life lost in anger

Praying for myself to be as you know md even without a word spoken

Praying with wet prayers

Praying in the name of Jesus

Forty-One:

When comes those dark moments

When comes those dark moments
Something changed you
The voice inside you spoke
That darker spirit pulled
Then you gave in to the call
Self-inflicted hate took control
That is when you become a child of death
The future is no more
You curse God and embrace Satin
It wasn't always this way
There were days in the sun with laughter
There were plans made for a bright tomorrow
Then your sight was only on yourself
Pulling away for your own gain
Stepping over others you learn to lie, cheat, and yes, hate

You were on a path of power and success at the cost of others

Laughing an evil laugh riches seemed to come

Yet you wanted more and found a way to steal

Then the judgement came you were caught

No place to turn you were now called to pay for your wrongs

Two others would join you this day

Another just as evil as yourself and one who seems out of place

Yet here you were pulling yourself along with your cross up the hill

The place of the skull

A fitting end you think for the evil within you

The one man called Jesus was cursed by the holy men

Words lifted

Those same words of hate

In his last hours you listened to the cries of the people

Even your evil companion cursed him

Then you called out to your evil friend

We deserve this end

But this man is put to death for no evil

Then Jesus looked towards him and spoke

Today you will be with me in Paradise

Then as Jesus passed you were ready

That darkness inside was lifted

Your earthly body too gave up

But your spiritual body is lifted away

For you believed in him

This man called Jesus Christ

It is never too late

To call on the name of Jesus

Forty-Two:

Wonder As You Will

Wonder As We Will

There will be storms in life
Clouds will cover blue skies
Winds will blow coldly
Rains and thunder scream with anger
Our travels pull us ever onward
We build walls for shelter
Holding back, yet we find tears
Safe, yet something is missing
Lost in life with the wolves at the door
Our travels have brought us to this place
We have prospered well, yet have an empty heart
Our minds lift to our roots
Those simple times
The place we called home
Dreams of life change
Our days became years
Years now a lifetime
We close our eyes in those memories
We see again those old friends
Just as before they are there
We hear the ringing of bells from the old church

The mailbox stands by the roadside
Inside there is a letter
To the family, it is written
Words scratched in pen in ink
A name signed and stained with tears
It is a letter from your own hand
Written long ago
Just a few words it held
I'm coming home

As you go through the travels of this book. If you have replies or thoughts, please feel free to express them. mkelley1950s@hotmail.com

About Mike Kelley

The Author Born in Kentucky's Bluegrass in 1945 life has opened its doors to the hand that follows now a Greater Spirit in that with which finds its ink to the pages. Having had a wild ride and range of schooling from advanced classes and studies, he holds a BA in Journalism but gives credit to his travels of the world and the coast to coast travels of the United States as his greatest teacher beyond that which comes of God himself.

A writer of poetry for those who don't like poetry and a writer of several short stories published, as well as three Christian books. From the early days of singing keys of a Remington Rand typewriter to the more modern methods, the development of his style remains untouched. His hobbies are in Art, of all kinds as nature's gifts

A Veteran of the Vietnam War, to the present time, now living in Isolation in Cincinnati, Ohio, with his wife Susan, but always one boot remaining in the mud of Kentucky's soil and the memories of the days of youth.

Reach Mike here at his Gmail or website

mkelley1950s@hotmail.com

Other Publications by Author

For Everything and Everyone There is a Season: By Mike Kelley & Mona Hess, Parables Publishing, ISBN 978-1-954308-84-8 Click Here

Hello God, It's Me Again: By Mike Kelley, Parables Publishing, ISBN 978-1-951497-02-6 Click Here

It's Me Again, Hello God, It's Me Again
By: Mike Kelley, Parables Publishing, ISBN 978-1951497-32-3

A Christmas Trilogy: By Mike Kelley,
Parables Publishing, ISBN 978-1-951497-77-4

In God's Hands, By Mike Kelley & Mona Hess, Parables Publishing, ISBN 978-1-951497-70-5

The River Cries: By Mike Kelley, Parables Publishing, ISBN 978-1-951497-93-4

Don't Listen to the Snakes: By Mike Kelley, available on Kindle. ALL BOOKS CLICK HERE

Mike Kelley would like to thank Samantha Fury for all of her help with his eBook formatting, Paperback, Hardback

Book Covers and uploading them to Amazon. She also helped Mike to start his website.

Here is a little more about Samantha Fury
Author, Design website formatting and more.

About Samantha Fury

www.samanthafury.com

Samantha Loves Romance. Her Street Justice Series is riveting, fun, full of romance, life struggles, a little detective work and humor when possible. Samantha also writes Romance under the pen name Samantha Lovern, you'll have to check out Sweet Prince, or the California Love Trilogy for more clean romance, here on Amazon.

Samantha was born in Kentucky, the daughter of a coal miner & his loving homemaker. She is an only child so she spent many hours using her imagination to keep her busy. She started writing when she was 8 and become a Christian that same year.

She works with many authors with formatting, book covers, advertising, uploading to amazon and building websites or tweaking them. You can learn much more about her books her and her groups, and more at her website. www.furycoverdesign.com

If you like this book check out more great books here

Christian Books in Multiple Genres, Join Christian Indie Author ~ Readers Group on Facebook. Opportunities to learn about great Christian authors.

https://www.facebook.com/groups/291215317668431/

Thanks For Reading

www.ingramcontent.com/pod-product-compliance
Lightning Source LLC
LaVergne TN
LVHW041104150826
845673LV00007B/1912

* 9 7 9 8 8 4 5 6 3 7 9 1 8 *